...on,
illustrated by Lisa Kopper

Books Beyond Words

Gaskell/St George's Hospital Medical School
LONDON

First published in Great Britain 1998 by St George's Hospital Medical School and Gaskell.

Text & illustration © Sheila Hollins 1998.

ISBN 1-901242-20-X

British Library Cataloguing-in-Publication Data.

A catalogue record for this book is available from the British Library.

Distributed in North America
by American Psychiatric Press, Inc.

ISBN 0-88048-590-6

Printed and bound in Great Britain by Acanthus Press Limited, Wellington, Somerset TA21 8ST.

Further information about the Books Beyond Words series can be obtained from:

Royal College of Psychiatrists   WM   829
17 Belgrave Square
London SW1X 8PG

Tel: 0171 235 2351
Fax: 0171 245 1231

Acknowledgements

We are grateful to many people who gave their time most generously to help us, in particular: Alan Corbett, Tamsin Cottis, Dorothea Duncan, Ruth Marchant, Wendy Perez, Raymond and Brenda Pope, Peter Raine, Heather Sequiera, Dr Eileen Vizard, Una Wallace.

Thanks also to the clients at Spring Hill: Centre for Young People with Developmental Disabilities, and to the staff at Blakes and Link Employment Agency and at Simmons House Adolescent Unit.

Finally, we are grateful to VOICE UK for having the idea for this project in the first place, and for approaching the Department of Health without whose generous financial support this book would not have been possible.

1

24

29

The following words are provided for readers or carers who want a ready-made story rather than make up their own.

Picture numbers

1. Susie lives here.
   She stirs the tea.

2. Susie washes up.

3. She watches TV with her friends.

4. She enjoys a bath at night-time.

5. And she likes reading in bed.
   But there is a man at the door. He is coming in.

6. She is scared! The man comes towards her.

7. He is going out of the room now.
   Susie is upset. Something bad has happened.

8. Karen knocks on the door in the morning to wake Susie.
   Susie is silent.

9. Susie sits on the edge of the bed. She wet the bed in the night. Karen sees that her bed is wet.

10. Susie shouts at everyone at breakfast.

11. Now she's alone in her bedroom. She feels awful.

12. She sits right in front of the TV. No one else can see.

13. Karen tries to move her.

14. Oh no! She's tearing her shirt off. Everyone is shocked. What is the matter with Susie?

15. Karen takes Susie to her room.

16. Karen takes Susie for a walk. Susie looks very sad.

17. Karen wonders what the matter is.

18. Susie knocks over her drink.

19. Karen tells her off. Anna sees it all happen.

20. They go to a clinic. The receptionist says hello.

21. Claire shows her where to sit. She listens to Susie.

22. Susie arrives at the clinic again.
    She sees Claire regularly.

23. Susie draws pictures about what happened.

24. Susie shows Claire what happened.

25. Susie thinks about the man who came in her bedroom. She's upset.

26. She's brushing her hair at home. She can't stop remembering.

27. Karen comforts her.

28. Susie sees Claire again. She is angry with the man.

29. Susie and Claire meet a policewoman and some other people. They explain what the man did to Susie. She tells them the name of the man.

30. Susie asks if the police will take the man away.

31. Susie doesn't think about the man so much.

32. Susie is fast asleep. Sometimes she dreams about the man. Usually she doesn't.
    She wakes up in the morning. She feels safer now.

33. Susie enjoys a biscuit.

34. Susie's with her friends.

I Can Get Through It

This book tells the story of a woman with learning disabilities. She is attacked by a man. We learn what happens to her and how she gets help.

Sadly, a lot of people are sexually abused, perhaps as many as 1500 every year just in the UK. It can happen anywhere – in someone's home, in a hostel or residential home, at a day centre or a social club, on transport or wherever people with learning disabilities are. Typically the abuse is by someone known to the victim, and it is not an isolated incident. The book shows that it is possible to find help and 'get through it'.

One very worrying fact is that often the person accused of hurting the man or woman with learning disabilities is not made to appear in court. This may be because the police and the lawyers do not think they can find enough evidence or they do not think that the person with learning disabilities would be able to appear in court and be a good witness. This does not mean that the person with learning disabilities is not telling the truth.

There are lots of improvements that need to be made to help people with learning or communication disabilities look after themselves and know what to do. Psychotherapy is one of the things which has been shown to help people who have been abused.

Post-Abuse Treatment

Psychotherapy

Many children and adults who are struggling to make sense of a difficulty in their lives are finding themselves helped by a talking and listening treatment – one of the many kinds of psychotherapy and counselling available in the NHS (National Health Service), as well as privately. It is very important that children and adults with learning and communication disabilities have the same access to treatment that other citizens do.

What is a talking treatment?

Even those of us with no speech are part of the world of language. We hear and understand something in words. Psychotherapy is an attempt, with words, to help make sense of the problems we carry inside us and show to others through our behaviour, our feelings and our language – both verbal and non-verbal.

All such treatments, whether carried out by an NHS nurse, psychologist, social worker or psychiatrist who have received extra training in psychotherapy, or by trained psychotherapists who are approved by the BCP (British Confederation of Psychotherapists) or UKCP (United Kingdom Council for Psychotherapy) use words as the main way of communicating, even if the person does not speak or use signs. Sometimes a person may need other help at the same time as therapy, e.g. medication or extra support at home.

With some adults with severe physical and/or learning disabilities, the therapist includes drawing materials and a range of objects that add to communication ability. For example, Sara Jones, aged 40, is a woman with a severe learning disability and physical disabilities too. She became depressed after a fall on her bathroom floor. She had no spoken speech and understood little language. However, because her therapist included a doll's house complete with furniture, she was able to demonstrate the act of falling over in the bathroom.

Who needs treatment?

Some families and individuals have long-standing deep problems but would never go for help, and some people go for help quickly. It is their own feelings that tell them whether they can untangle the worry by themselves. It is important to remember that while love and friendship both help, they cannot take away all emotional pain. Similarly, you cannot love someone out of an emotional problem or deep distress. You can support somebody and that makes a big difference. But there is an untangling process that may have to be done with someone else who is not involved.

How to get therapy?

First, the person has to feel that there is a problem they need help with. Second, they have to be able to tell someone that they would like help in understanding a problem. Depending on somebody's age, the people to tell could include their parents, teachers, a keyworker, a social worker, psychiatrist, a general practitioner (GP) or someone from their church, mosque or synagogue if they are religious.

Once a letter is sent to the person's local psychotherapy service from their GP they will then wait for an appointment letter. Once this arrives the person will have from one to three meetings to explore their problem and see if they and the therapist think it would be a good idea to start psychotherapy. It may not be with the person who they first meet.

What happens in therapy?

For all talking therapies in the NHS, people see the same person in the same room at the same time each week. Sometimes the person might not be able to go because they are not well or have to go somewhere else. Very occasionally the therapist may have to miss a session. Every few months there is another holiday – Christmas, Easter or Summer – and people miss therapy. However, because it is the same place and time almost every week, people build up a sense of safety and security in which it is possible to discuss their problems. In a talking therapy the therapist will only speak about subjects the person raises. It may be that the person does not want to talk about their particular problem and has other things on their mind. That is fine. Everything the person says or does is valued and will be thought about.

Usually, children and adults find it helpful to talk about their worries a little bit, once they feel safe with the therapist.

While our research shows that children and adults with learning disabilities, like everyone else, feel better as a result of therapy, therapy is not always easy. It can be painful remembering and talking about difficult things that have happened in your life. 'Getting through' sexual abuse will not be quick. People will need time and they may have ups and downs. However, there are important emotional rewards for people entering this treatment, including managing their life and feelings more easily. They may need help to go to their therapy sessions. Their supporters will need to understand that the person's sessions are private even if the person is upset before or after the sessions. Supporters will also need to remember that therapy cannot be the sole source of support.

Do people need therapy when they are sexually abused?

Sexual abuse is a betrayal of mind and body. Although it causes physical and emotional problems, not everyone needs treatment. Susan, aged 14, was abused by the driver who took her to her club. She told her mother the moment she got home and her mother believed her and called the police immediately. Although the case did not get to court, the fact that her mother had believed her right away had a big impact on Susan and she said she did not need to talk to anyone else about it.

Henry, aged 22, told his mother he had been abused by his grandfather. She was shocked and furious, and said he was a liar. Henry got sadder and sadder and did not even have the energy to eat. His GP got worried and arranged for therapy.

In other words, it is not just the fact that abuse has happened that makes someone need therapy, it is how it is dealt with by people close to them, and the individual's own personal resources.

Where to go for help and advice

VOICE UK is a support and information group for people with learning disabilities who have been abused and hurt, and for their families and carers. VOICE has a telephone service and tries to answer questions and help people with their problems. Meetings for parents are held in London, as well as teleconferences (telephone calls that link people all over the country). VOICE sends out a newsletter three times a year which tells how other families are coping, as well as giving information about what is happening about services for people with learning disabilities. Some parents who first approached VOICE for help are now helping other parents. These are called Parent Contact Points and they will talk with 'new' parents who have just found out about what has happened to their son or daughter and feel that their world has been shattered.

VOICE UK is based at PO Box 238, Derby DE1 9PN (Tel: 01332 519872).

Written Information

Parents Against Abuse. Book written with the help of parents whose son or daughter has been abused. Helps parents with strategies on how to prevent abuse and how to cope if it has occurred. Free to VOICE members, £3.50 to others. Available from VOICE UK, address as above.

How to Avoid Abuse (working title). Joint leaflet from VOICE UK and CHANGE. Available from Spring 1999.

Action Against Abuse. Recognising and preventing abuse of people with learning disabilities. For service users and supporters and families. Available from the Association for Residential Care, ARC House, Marsden Street, Chesterfield S40 1JY (Tel: 01246 555043). Price for three packs £35.00 (inc. p. & p.), ARC members, £28.00. Service users pack £10.00 (inc. p. & p.).

There are three other related titles in the Books Beyond Words series which are available at £10.00 each (inc. p. & p.) from the Royal College of Psychiatrists, 17 Belgrave Square, London SW1X 8PG (Tel: 0171 235 2351).

Bob Tells All and *Jenny Speaks Out* by Sheila Hollins and Valerie Sinason. With the help of these two companion volumes, people with communication difficulties can be helped to open up about their experience of sexual abuse.

Going to Court by Sheila Hollins, Valerie Sinason and Julie Boniface. About being a witness in court.

Organisations providing training or offering therapy and counselling

British Confederation of Psychotherapists (BCP)

37 Mapesbury Road   **Tel: 0181 830 5173**
London NW2 4HJ

The BCP is an association of psychoanalysts, analytical psychologists and psychoanalytic psychotherapists. Members have their roots in psychoanalysis and psychoanalytic psychotherapy. All have had substantial postgraduate training. It publishes a register of its members and their geographical location.

United Kingdom Council for Psychotherapy (UKCP)

167–169 Great Portland Street   **Tel: 0171 436 3002**
London W1N 5FB

The UKCP has the substantial aim of creating a broadly based profession of psychotherapy that would be as well organised as other traditional professions. It is the largest umbrella organisation. It maintains and publishes a register of its members and their geographical location.

British Psychological Society   **Tel: 01162 549568**

St Andrews House
48 Princess Road East
Leicester LE1 7DR

The British Psychological Society is the professional body for all qualified psychologists and maintains a register of its members.

Royal College of Psychiatrists   Tel: 0171 235 2351

17 Belgrave Square
London SW1X 8PG

The Royal College of Psychiatrists is the professional body concerned with accrediting training for psychiatrists, and maintaining professional standards. It has a Faculty of Psychiatry of Learning Disability.

British Association of Counselling   Tel: 01788 578328

1 Regents Place
Rugby
Coventry CV21 2PJ

The British Association of Counselling maintains the register of all trained counsellors in the UK.

Respond   Tel: 0171 383 0700

3rd Floor
24–32 Stephenson Way
London NW1 2HD

Offers assessment and treatment to people with learning disabilities who are victims and/or perpetrators of sexual abuse, and advice, training and consultancy to carers and professionals.

If an organisation says that it does not offer psycho-therapy or counselling to people with learning disabilities who have been abused, it is extremely important that parents, carers and supporters should insist on the ethical right of the abused person to have access to assessment and treatment services. Such treatment has been proved to be both necessary and effective.